WELCOME TO
PASSPORT TO READING
A beginning reader's ticket to a brand-new world!

Every book in this program is designed to build read-along and read-alone skills, level by level, through engaging and enriching stories. As the reader turns each page, he or she will become more confident with new vocabulary, sight words, and comprehension.

These PASSPORT TO READING levels will help you choose the perfect book for every reader.

READING TOGETHER
Read short words in simple sentence structures together to begin a reader's journey.

READING OUT LOUD
Encourage developing readers to sound out words in more complex stories with simple vocabulary.

READING INDEPENDENTLY
Newly independent readers gain confidence reading more complex sentences with higher word counts.

READY TO READ MORE
Readers prepare for chapter books with fewer illustrations and longer paragraphs.

This book features sight words from the educator-supported Dolch Sight Words List. This encourages the reader to recognize commonly used vocabulary words, increasing reading speed and fluency.

For more information, please visit passporttoreadingbooks.com.

Enjoy the journey!

Little, Brown and Company
Hachette Book Group
1290 Avenue of the Americas, New York, NY 10104
Visit us at LBYR.com

First Edition: October 2019

Little, Brown and Company is a division of Hachette Book Group, Inc. The Little, Brown name and logo are trademarks of Hachette Book Group, Inc.

The publisher is not responsible for websites (or their content) that are not owned by the publisher.

Library of Congress Control Number 2019944221

ISBNs: 978-0-316-49099-3 (pbk.), 978-0-316-49101-3 (ebook), 978-0-316-49102-0 (ebook), 978-0-316-49098-6 (ebook)

Printed in the United States of America

CW

10 9 8 7 6 5 4 3 2 1

Passport to Reading titles are leveled by independent reviewers applying the standards developed by Irene Fountas and Gay Su Pinnell in *Matching Books to Readers: Using Leveled Books in Guided Reading*, Heinemann, 1999.

OFFICIAL
MARK OF
SPIRIT

𝓡𝒾𝓅𝓁𝑒𝓎® **Readers**

All true and unbelievable!

Learning to read. Reading to learn!

LEVEL ONE Sounding It Out Preschool–Kindergarten
For kids who know their alphabet and are starting to sound out words.

learning sight words • beginning reading • sounding out words

LEVEL TWO Reading with Help Preschool–Grade 1
For kids who know sight words and are learning to sound out new words.

expanding vocabulary • building confidence • sounding out bigger words

LEVEL THREE Independent Reading Grades 1–3
For kids who are beginning to read on their own.

introducing paragraphs • challenging vocabulary • reading for comprehension

LEVEL FOUR Chapters Grades 2–4
For confident readers who enjoy a mixture of images and story.

reading for learning • more complex content • feeding curiosity

Ripley Readers Designed to help kids build their reading skills and confidence at any level, this program offers a variety of fun, entertaining, and unbelievable topics to interest even the most reluctant readers. With stories and information that will spark their curiosity, each book will motivate them to start and keep reading.

Vice President, Licensing & Publishing Amanda Joiner
Editorial Manager Carrie Bolin

Editor Jessica Firpi
Writer Korynn Freels
Designer Rose Audette

Published by Ripley Publishing 2019

10 9 8 7 6 5 4 3 2 1

Copyright © 2019 Ripley Publishing

ISBN: 978-1-60991-324-3

For more information regarding permission, contact:
VP Licensing & Publishing
Ripley Entertainment Inc.
7576 Kingspointe Parkway, Suite 188
Orlando, Florida 32819

Email: publishing@ripleys.com
www.ripleys.com/books
Manufactured in China in June 2019.

First Printing

Library of Congress Control Number: 2019942264

PUBLISHER'S NOTE
While every effort has been made to verify the accuracy of the entries in this book, the Publisher cannot be held responsible for any errors contained in the work. They would be glad to receive any information from readers.

DREAMWORKS

Spirit

RIDING FREE

Merry Christmas!

by Jennifer Fox

LITTLE, BROWN AND COMPANY
New York   Boston

Attention, Spirit Riding Free fans!
Look for these words
when you read this book.
Can you spot them all?

slippery

frozen

crack

lasso

It is almost Christmastime in Miradero.

Christmas is Lucky's favorite
time of year!

This is Lucky's first Christmas
in Miradero.
There is not a lot of snow!
That is okay because the whole
town is decorated.

There is also a big green tree
in the middle of Miradero.
It has many brightly colored lights.

Back in the city, Lucky and her dad looked at all the fancy store window displays every winter.

She cannot do that this year.

Sometimes Lucky misses
living in the city.

Lucky meets her friends for a winter trail ride.

Pru, Abigail, and Lucky are the PALs. Being with her pals always makes Lucky feel good.

The PALs love riding
their horses together.
Today, they decide to take Spirit,
Chica Linda, and Boomerang into
the snowy mountains.

"Easy, Spirit," Lucky says to her horse.

The trail has ice on it.

Spirit tries not to slide.

He is not used to the ground

being so slippery.

Abigail is so excited.

She says, "The whole world is
covered in ice!"

The ice is very pretty,
but it can be dangerous, too.

The PALs need to be careful.

While on the trail, the PALs hear
someone shout.

"Help!" the voice calls.

A young girl is stuck in the
middle of a frozen lake.

The ice is too thin to hold her.

It starts to crack!

"Hang on!" shouts Lucky.
She walks slowly onto the ice.

"I am Lucky," she says calmly.
"You should not worry.
Everything will be okay."

Pru throws her lasso around the girl.

The PALs pull her to safety!

On the way back to Miradero,
a snowstorm starts.
The PALs learn that the trains
are stuck in the mountains.
They cannot get to town.

"Santa will not be able to visit
in this snow," Snips cries.
"That means no presents!"
Snips is very sad.

The PALs come up with
a plan to save Christmas.

"We can be Santa's helpers,"
says Lucky.

Abigail, Pru, and Lucky
make special gifts.
They will give the gifts to all
the children in Miradero.

The PALs wait until nighttime.
Everyone else has to be asleep
for their plan to work!

Lucky, Abigail, and Pru sneak through
Miradero to deliver the presents.

Chica Linda, Spirit, and
Boomerang help, too!

Everyone in Miradero wakes up
on Christmas morning.
The children are so excited
about their special gifts!

Maricela gets a beautiful new dress.

Turo gets a blanket for his horse, Junipero.

Even Spirit receives special presents.

The PALs give him hay and apples
for his herd.

Lucky gets a special gift from
Pru and Abigail, too.

Sometimes Lucky misses the city.
But this Christmas, she is exactly
where she wants to be.
She is in Miradero with Spirit
and her PALs.